PUNCHINELLO AND THE
Most Marvelous Gift

ILLUSTRATIONS BY SERGIO MARTINEZ

MAX LUCADO

SCHOLASTIC INC.

New York Toronto London Auckland Sydney
Mexico City New Delhi Hong Kong Buenos Aires

ISBN 0-439-72408-2

12 11 10 9 8 7 6 5 4 3 2   5 6 7 8 9 10/0

Printed in the U.S.A.   23

First Scholastic printing, October 2005
Edited by Karen Hill
Design: UDG | DesignWorks, www.udgdesignworks.com
The author extends special appreciation to Greg Perkins for the great idea.

FOR
JEFF, CAROL, CHRISTOPHER, AND NATALEIGH NELSON

For bringing so much marvelous music into our world, thank you.
May your Maker fill your lives with more.

PUNCHINELLO'S FEET DANGLED from Eli's workbench.

"This is my favorite time of the year, Eli. I love Maker-Day."

"That's great." The big-handed woodworker smiled as he swept the sawdust from the floor. "I love being your maker."

"This year I want to do something really big for you."

"You do?" Eli paused and asked, "Like what?"

"I don't know yet, but I'll think of something."

"Just being with you is enough for me, Punchinello," the woodcarver told him.

"But I want to do more. I like you. I love you! I want all to see—without you, Eli, there'd be no me!" The little Wemmick's eyes grew wide. "Hey, that rhymes!"

He jumped off the bench and gave his maker a big hug. "Just wait, Eli. This year I'm doing something really big for you." He scampered out the door, making a song out of the words he had just said:

"I like you.
I love you.
I want all to see—
without you, Eli,
there'd be no me."

"Be careful, little friend." Eli smiled and waved.

Punchinello sang his new song all the way to Wemmicksville. The village was bustling. Wemmicks packed the streets and shops. Everyone was getting ready for the big day. The Wee Wemmick choir rehearsed in the village square. Workers were putting up the town tree. Some townspeople shopped; others painted windows. Everyone smiled. Maker-Day made everyone happy.

And Maker-Day made Hans, the baker, busy! Busy baking a seven-layer version of his famous chocolate cherry truffle cake with double butter-cream frosting. Punchinello loved to visit his squatty friend with the starched hat. He peeked into the window of the bakery to see Hans tippy-toed on the top step of a tall ladder, placing cherries around the seventh layer. The cake nearly touched the ceiling. Punchinello smacked his lips and stepped into the doorway.

"Hi, Hans!" Punchinello called. The baker jumped, and the ladder began to sway. Back-back-back, until Hans yanked himself and the ladder forward and started falling toward the cake. *Oh, no!* Hans would have plunged right into it, but Punchinello dashed across the room, scampered up the ladder, and grabbed the baker by the collar.

"Whew!" Hans sighed, his face within licking distance of the frosting.

"I'm sorry," Punchinello apologized.

"No problem, little friend," Hans replied as he climbed down the ladder. "My mind was on the cake." He turned, placed his hands on his hips, and beamed. "Isn't it something? Triumphant truffles! My cake is going to be the best part of the Maker-Day Festival."

"Really?"

"Definitely. The very best part. Now, if you'll hand me that jar of cherries . . ." Punchinello did. Hans climbed the ladder.

Punchinello decided to see what else was happening in Wemmicksville. "See you later, Hans!" But the busy baker didn't hear. His mind was on the cherries.

And at the next shop Violet's mind was on flowers. Her bouquet stood taller than her entire flower shop. But where was the florist?

"I've never seen so many flowers," Punchinello said to himself.

"Do you like it?" asked a voice from deep within the mountain of flowers. Violet peeked at Punch through the daisies.

"I think I do. But it's so big I can't see it all."

"It's the biggest bouquet in the history of Wemmicksville," Violet boasted as she placed a red carnation next to a white tulip.

"What's it for?"

"Maker-Day, of course. My beautiful bouquet will be the best part of tomorrow's Maker-Day Festival."

"But . . . Hans just told me . . ."

Violet glared at him. "Hans and his cake? Hah! Eli will like my flowers better than that baker's stack of dough."

She lifted her chin and turned back to the bouquet.

"Oh." Punchinello swallowed. "I think I'll move on."

He stepped around the flowers into the street, bumping into his friend Lucia, who was reading a sheet of music.

"Happy Maker-Day, Lucia."

"Same to you, Punch. I'm late for my voice lesson."

"Voice lesson?"

"I'm going to sing a solo at the Maker-Day Festival. My song is going to make this the best Maker-Day ever!"

"But Hans and Violet just said—"

Lucia never heard him. "Dr. Marvel is training me. He will accompany me on his Marvellaphony-organoni."

"I made up a song today—," Punchinello started, but then he stopped. "Marvella-*what?*"

"Come on. I'll show you. But we have to hurry. I can't keep Dr. Marvel waiting!"

Lucia grabbed Punchinello's hand and led him down the busy street. Past the toy store packed with little Wemmicks. Past the dress store window painted red and green. Past the huge Maker-Day tree standing in the middle of Wemmick Square.

Punchinello paused at the sight of the enormous tree. "Hey, let's add some decorations."

"We don't have time, Punch. Come on."

Around the corner they turned. The studio sat just off the main street. The sign over the door read, Dr. Marvel's Music Manufactory.

The moment they closed the door, the two friends heard music erupt in the big room. Trumpets blared. Flutes whistled. Drums ka-boomed, and tubas bellowed. Punchinello looked around for a marching band. When he didn't see one, he ducked behind Lucia. "Don't be afraid," she said. "It's the Marvellaphony-organoni."

She motioned toward the huge contraption that took up the back half of the studio. Punchinello had never seen anything like it. In the center sat a piano. Two saxophones hung from one side and a bass drum from the other. Five flutes dangled from the drum. Trumpets stuck out above the piano, and a mechanical arm banged a spoon on a pot. On the very top a fishing line yanked the clapper of a bell, a train whistle tooted, and trombones played in turn.

Looking small in front of it all, sat Dr. Marvel. His hands raced back and forth between the piano keyboard and a large panel of buttons, switches, and levers—each with a sign: Louder, Softer, More Beep, Big Booms, Pull for Taps, Tug for Toots. His feet moved even faster; one pumped air into the instruments. The other foot pressed the bass drum pedal. The musician was in nonstop motion.

"Doctor," Lucia called loudly (but not loudly enough).

"Dr. Marvel!" she shouted. He still didn't turn.

"Dr. Marvel!!!" she and Punchinello yelled together at the top of their lungs. The music came to a sudden stop, and the stumpy little Wemmick turned his head.

When he saw Lucia, his thick eyebrows lifted, and he peered over his glasses. "Why, come in, come in! And who is your friend?"

"This is Punchinello."

"Hello, Funny-Pillow. Please come in and rest.
Isn't my music machine the absolute best?"

"Uh, my name is *Punchinello.* I've never seen anything like your machine."

"And you never will—did you hear it bellow?
This invention is one of a kind, Marshy-Mallow."

"Punch*inello,*" Punch said, glancing at Lucia. She just shrugged.

Dr. Marvel didn't hear. He had turned to Lucia.

"And now, my dear, have you come to sing?
Together you and I will make Maker-Day ring!"

"I've been practicing my song," Lucia chimed in.

Punchinello spoke up. "Hey, speaking of songs, I made one up for Eli."

But neither Dr. Marvel nor Lucia listened. They were already tuning up the Marvellaphony-organoni, leaving Punchinello standing alone.

He stepped outside. "Maker-Day is almost here, and I still don't know what I'm going to do for Eli."

Just having you with me is enough, Punchinello remembered his maker saying. But he still wanted to give Eli a special gift. All the way home, he tried to think of an idea.

The next morning he was still thinking about the gift for Eli. With hands deep in his pockets, Punchinello talked to himself all the way to Wemmicksville. "Maybe I could bake a Wemberry pie." Then he remembered how awful his last pie tasted. "Naw, I can't cook. What if I make a bouquet for Eli?" Then he remembered the size of Violet's flower arrangement. "I could never make one that big," Punch said.

Punchinello had no idea what to do. It was Maker-Day, and he had no gift to give his maker.

Main Street overflowed with Wemmicks. Every wooden person in Wemmick Valley was pressing toward the town square where a large circle had been roped off. In the center of the circle the Maker-Day tree sparkled. The mayor and his wife stood on a large platform. Before them were three large objects hidden under pieces of canvas. Punchinello knew exactly what they were.

Violet stood next to one, Hans beside the other. Lucia paced between them, back and forth in front of the covered music machine. She looked worried. Dr. Marvel was nowhere to be seen.

Punchinello caught her attention. "Lucia," he shouted, "where's Dr. Marvel?"

She looked over her shoulder toward the blanketed instrument. That's when Punchinello saw the moving bumps under the cover. "Something is broken," she said.

Before Punchinello could ask more, the mayor and his wife stepped in front of the huge Maker-Day Festival sign, tapped on the microphone, and announced: "Happy Maker-Day, everyone!"

The crowd cheered.

Unrolling a big scroll, the mayor began to read a very boring speech: "Being that this is Maker-Day and we are made by our maker, I hereby and so forth with henceforth pleasure . . ."

Punch noticed Dr. Marvel peeking out from under the cover, motioning to Lucia. She leaned over; he whispered, and she turned red. She whispered back, and Punchinello knew something was wrong.

That's when they looked at him. Lucia motioned for him to come over. He crawled under the ropes.

"You've got to help us. The air-pumper is stuck. Dr. Marvel needs you to run the controls while he keeps it working."

"But I don't know how to—"

"It's easy," she interrupted. "Just sit on his shoulders and do what he says." The music professor nodded.

About that time, the crowd began to cheer again. The mayor had presented Violet and her flowers. The three stopped whispering long enough to see her curtsy in front of the bouquet.

"The best part of Maker-Day!" shouted the mayor.

"O, no, it's not!" screamed Hans. He was already on the top step of his ladder. At a wave of his hand, a rope was yanked, and the canvas pulled straight up, unveiling his seven-layer chocolate cherry truffle cake with double butter-cream frosting.

The townspeople gasped, then roared in approval. Violet crossed her arms and frowned, and Dr. Marvel motioned to Punchinello.

> *"Come on, Runny-Jello, it's time to play.*
> *We'll be the best part of this Maker-Day."*

The musician sat on the bench. Punch climbed on his shoulders, and Lucia stood with her back to them, interlocked her fingers, pointed her elbows to either side, and prepared to sing.

Punchinello stared at all the buttons. He gulped and thought to himself, *How will I ever do this?* There were so many of them: Big Blast, Soft Windy Sound, Bells Tinkling, Harps Singing . . .

"I don't think I can do—"

Before Punchinello could finish, Dr. Marvel called him into action.

"Honey-Mellow, let's get flashing.
Pull the lever that reads, Cymbal Clashing."
Punchinello looked frantically, spotted the lever, and gave it a pull. Mechanical
hands lifted a set of cymbals, and "crash!" the song began. Lucia started singing, her
voice warbling up and down as if someone were shaking her. Thinking she was sick,
Punchinello looked over his shoulder. But Lucia wasn't sick. "Why are you
making that noise?" he hollered at her.
"Pasty-Fellow, for chitchat we have no time!
Reach to the right and give me a chime!"
Punchinello pulled the rope bell and felt the music professor bouncing beneath
him, pushing doubly hard on the air pump. Instruments came alive, blasting and
blowing, surrounding Punchinello in a hurricane of music. Dr. Marvel kept
shouting instructions as Punch pushed buttons.
"A blast from the tuba, now strings from the cello.
Keep alert up there, Funny-Fellow."
"My name is *Punchinello!*" the lever-yanking Wemmick yelled. He leaned
down so his voice would be heard. He never should have lowered his head.
His forehead hit the lever labeled, Let Her Go! And the Marvellaphony-organoni
started to rumble. Wemmicks grabbed their children and covered their ears.

The earthquaking platform shook the mayor out of his chair. Decorations fell from the Maker-Day tree. Lucia stopped singing. The professor started shouting,

"Turn it down; she's starting to shake!
The last thing we want is for this thing to break!"

It was too late. The train whistle flew first, blasting off the Marvellaphony-organoni like a skyrocket. The trombones were next to go. Then the saxophones. With the boom of a kettledrum, everything else exploded. Flutes flew, and cymbals sailed. Punch and the professor were doing all they could do, flipping switches, pulling ropes, but nothing helped. Dr. Marvel should have stopped pumping, but for some odd reason, he pumped harder than ever. And since there were no instruments, the air blasted through the bouncing hose right at Hans's seven-layer chocolate cake, blowing icing and cherries all over the Wemmicks.

Lucia grabbed the flopping hose and yanked it away from the cake but accidentally aimed it in the direction of Violet's bouquet. The air suddenly filled with flowers. Petals rained down on the already sticky, cake-covered Wemmicks. The villagers were stunned. One minute they were ducking flying French horns; the next they were showered with cake and carnations.

Then, in an instant, the pandemonium stopped. The town square was quiet, the Wemmicks in shock from the explosion.

"Armi-Dillow, my friend, may I tell you somethin'?
It looks to me like you pushed the wrong button."

Hans and Violet wiped clumps of dough from their eyes. The mayor and his wife looked like snow creatures, covered with cake frosting from head to toe. Only Lucia, the professor, and Punchinello were uncaked and unpetaled. For a long time no one moved.

No one knew what to say.

That's when they heard the flute—a single, small, sweet-sounding flute. A little girl, standing next to the tree, hair sticky with cake, was playing it. At first she didn't notice everyone looking. But when she did, she stopped.

"I'm sorry." She blushed. "It landed in my lap."

"Please," Punchinello pleaded, "keep playing." Everyone nodded. The soft flute sounded nice after the bellowing Marvellaphony-organoni. Not far from the girl, an old Wemmick picked up a violin and began to play. Another villager, familiar with clarinets, found one and played along. Within a matter of moments, a dozen musicians were serenading the townspeople with their music.

Dr. Marvel sighed with relief. Lucia smiled, and Punchinello raised his hand and announced, "Hey, every Wemmick . . . I've got a great idea!"

Eli was hard at work when he heard the music. The sound was so sweet, it made him put down his hammer and lean out the window of his workshop. Looking down the hill, he saw the long line of Wemmicks. He listened with his whole heart to the words of the song. Some played it. Some sang it. Everyone meant it.

> *"We like you.*
> *We love you.*
> *We all agree—*
> *Without you, Eli,*
> *there'd be no we."*

When all the Wemmicks had gathered before him, Eli had to smile. The town made quite a choir—cake-covered, flower-colored, and smiling like they'd never had so much fun. They sang the verse over and over until finally they stopped and applauded for Eli.

And he clapped for them.

"What a most marvelous song," he thanked them, "and what a most marvelous gift."

Dr. Marvel spoke up in agreement. .

> *"Mellow-Yellow, my friend, this moment I must say,*
> *is, without a doubt, the best of Maker-Day."*

The people applauded. Lucia nodded. Punchinello just blushed.